A SHORT STORY

PIGGY

HOLLY KNIGHTLEY
A SHORT STORY
PIGGY

ISBN: 978-1-958761-76-2

For Anastasia and Dimitri

CONTENTS

CHAPTER ONE

The Three Little Pigs

"**I**t's not going to bite you," Blake said, swallowing a laugh.

My eyes cut to him, my voice coming out in a hiss. "Famous last words." He knew I couldn't just pick it up. Whether it was a five-dollar bill or a hundred-dollar bill, I couldn't break my routine that easily.

My life was like *Groundhog Day*—the movie, that is. Every day I did the same thing. I'm not complaining; I like it like that. I *needed* it like that. You could set your clock to my daily routine. Who needs modern technology, or sundials, or crystal balls, or heck, a groundhog, when Alley Faye was around?

When Blake got home from work, we'd head to Batsto Village—the best national park, as far as I'm concerned. We'd walk our loop around the historical town, wrapping around the front of the mansion, before heading back to the parking lot. When I got home, I showered. Then we ate dinner. Routine. Routine. Routine.

After staring at a computer screen all day answering customer service complaints for Harrah's Resorts and Casino, our walk was easily my favorite part of my self-induced *Groundhog Day*. We saw a lot of the same people walking the loop for exercise, like the Wallaces, and then there was my ex-boyfriend, Billy, selling Italian ice, popcorn and pretzels, hotdogs and French fries, along with a few beverage options out of his food truck in the parking lot. There was just enough variation in the regulars of the park to let me know I wasn't trapped in some virtual reality *Matrix.*

One thing I didn't do as part of my daily routine was pick up stray money. It just wasn't something that I did. So, when I saw a five-dollar bill on the ground, I had to think about it. I'm autistic. I have the kind of autism that parallels OCD and dictates I do everything on routine. This need to do things in the order I think they should be done in has gotten worse. It's always getting worse. The older I get, the harder it is for me to be flexible. I felt as rigid as a rawhide bone these days as I struggled with hiccups in my routine.

The likelihood of picking up the five-dollar bill out of the visitor center's flower bed and Honest Abe biting my hand off was slim to none, but still, picking up the money could be biting off more than I could chew. If I wasn't careful, it could wrinkle my mood, set me off—that is—if I didn't think about it.

Blake knew this, after almost two years together; he better know how I am. I suppose that's why a smile tugged on his lips. He was the proverbial normal. He didn't understand. He thought my quirks, as he called them, were funny.

I wish they were to me. Anything that strayed from my regular routine, I had to visualize doing, and what doing *it* would mean for my day. This probably sounds crazy to a *normal* person but it's how my brain works. It all happens relatively quickly. Like in this instance, I wasn't staring at the money on the ground for hours or anything like that. My response time was just delayed. The average person would have picked up the money without a second's hesitation. That's where I differ. I paused to think. I just couldn't be reflexive about it, that's all.

"Want me to pick it up?" Blake asked.

I toed the facedown five, nudging it with my sneaker. "No, I got it," I said, ultimately picking the five-dollar bill off the ground.

"Now, was that so hard?" Blake quizzed.

If looks could kill, I'm afraid I would've killed my fiancé right then and there. His body would've crumbled in the daffodils, but I don't think the landscaper would have minded. Blake would quite literally be pushing up daisies in no time.

"I'm not a child, Blake," I said to my still very alive fiancé, as if his name was a profanity that would make a sailor blush. I loathed it when he said things like that. It made me seethe from the inside out until I became the Incredible Hulk and needed to smash things. Nothing is worse than being made to feel silly for things you can't control. Every time he gave me these mental pats-on-the-back, I felt like he was patronizing me. He wasn't, I knew he wasn't, but it sure felt like that.

"No, you're not a baby, *but* you're my *baby*," he cooed.

Tucking my dark hair behind my ears like I meant business, I corrected him, "I'm your fiancé."

He pressed a kiss to my cheek. "And my baby."

Pointing to my belly, my figurative Hulk muscles deflating, I said, "No, these are your babies." Blake was as surprised as I was when the doctor told us we were having twins, a boy and a girl, but sometimes life happens like that. We decided against the Luke and Leia thing, or a mashed-up concoction of the *Star Wars* twins, despite my father's constant pitches. In honor of the classic comedy duo, Laurel and Hardy, the Durwood twins would dutifully be named Laurel and Harvey. My poor children, they didn't stand a chance of being normal with me as their mother. Thank goodness for Blake.

"Better put that away for a rainy day," Blake said to me, inclining his chin to the five-dollar bill in my hand.

My skin felt tight. I knew I had to put it away. I didn't need his constant direction, but that was Blake for you. I faked a smile.

Autistic people are really good at faking things. It's how we blend into the mundane, how we learn to hide in plain sight, a term known in the autism community as *masking*. Somedays, I felt like the serial killer Dexter, from TV. I related to Dexter's journey of learning to act *human* on so many levels.

Blake smiled back at me as if I had just accepted another marriage proposal. He could be so oblivious, but he was always very handsome amidst being clueless. It was part of his charm.

Going to place the money in my fanny pack, I realized Abraham Lincoln had been defaced with a pig nose. In place of cute round pig ears, devil horns sprouted from the crown of his head in calculated spikes. Next to his iconic portrait, written in capital letters with a black marker was a message. As I read it, my pulse slowed to a crawl, my blood like ice in my veins: *HERE PIGGY, PIGGY, PIGGY. GREED IS A SIN, AND YOU JUST LET ME IN.*

"What's wrong?" Blake asked when I didn't put the money in my wallet.

"Someone drew on it."

He took it from me, a burst of laughter sounding off like a bomb between my ears.

"What's funny?" I asked, genuinely confused by his sudden hysterics.

"The saying. It's from that old nursery rhyme. You know, *The Three Little Pigs?*"

"I don't recall the three little pigs letting sin in, or the Big Bad Wolf, for that matter. He blows their houses down. Well, two of the three, that is."

"It's metaphorical," Blake said with a smug smile that showed off the dimple in his chin.

"You're a cop, not a literary major, so chill with that. And some friendly advice, Officer Durwood, from a concerned mother-to-be, you might want to brush up on the fairy tales before the twins get here."

"I have time," he countered, as if I had just insulted his ability to be a good father.

He did. The twins weren't due to arrive for months—five months to be exact. Our wedding, on the other hand, was less than two weeks away. My belly already looked like a snake after a ratatouille dinner. So much so, there was a real possibility the corset the seamstress added to the back of my dress wouldn't cut it. I was starting to think there was a possibility there were more than two little piggies in there; but as long as there wasn't five and they weren't going to the market before their due date, I'd be okay.

Honestly, Blake was better prepared for the twins than me. Amid the wedding preparations, I'd been slacking on the baby stuff. The nursery still wasn't done, chiefly because I couldn't decide on a color and yellow felt like a cop-out to me. To top that off, I wasn't an expert myself on fairy tales, Disney, or anything baby.

After reading the strange little message on the five-dollar bill, I thought I'd skip the story of the *Three Little Pigs*. I was pretty sure in some versions the wolf ate the first two piglets. I didn't want to give Laurel and Harvey nightmares, or me, for that matter. There was just something creepy about the message. Despite Blake's laughter, there was *nothing* funny about it. Whether it was metaphorical or not, it was just off, and I didn't like it.

I took the five from Blake and placed it back on the ground right where I found it.

"You're kidding me?" Blake said, quirking an eyebrow.

"Bad juju."

"Most people would think finding money on the ground was good luck."

Before I could defend my action, I heard a familiar voice. "Hi, Alley and Blake!"

"Hey, Mr. and Mrs. Wallace," I replied with my practiced

smile.

"What are you two doing?" Mr. Wallace asked, his eyes darting to the five-dollar bill by my feet. "A scavenger hunt or something?"

"No. I found that five, but someone wrote a nasty message on it, so I'm leaving it where I found it."

Mr. Wallace didn't bat an eye. He, like his wife, knew I was particular. I had grown up next to the Wallace family my whole life. Their big white house was the twin to my childhood home. I couldn't visit my parents without stopping in to say hello to the Wallaces. They were like a second set of grandparents, Mr. Wallace being the more accepting of the two.

"Can't have that, before the big day," Mrs. Wallace said loudly. It was evident she didn't have her hearing aids in. She patted her husband's belly and said with a wide smile that looked like it hurt, "We're trying to get a few pounds off by then."

I mirrored Mrs. Wallace and patted my own tummy. "I understand."

Everyone laughed, but I wasn't funny, nor was I trying to be. It's strange how people laugh at things that aren't humorous, more so than leaving money on the ground.

We said our goodbyes to the Wallaces and cut across the parking lot to Blake's SUV. My ritualistic wave to Billy out of the way, I opened the passenger side door and got in. My eyes gravitated to Mr. and Mrs. Wallace where they were still huddled around the five-dollar bill on the ground.

"Do you think he'll take it?" I asked.

Blake opened his car door as Mr. Wallace put the five in his pocket. "That's a yes," he said, stating the obvious.

"He let greed in," I muttered.

"Greed may be the Big Bad Wolf, Al, but it's just a five." His mouth turned up in a sideways smile, the dimple in his chin looking very Hollywood heartthrob. "It would take a lot more money to corrupt Mr. Wallace than that. So, I wouldn't worry about it. Some asshole kid wrote it to be prophetic."

I sighed, settling back into my seat. This little piggy wanted to go home.

CHAPTER TWO
Huff and Puff

"I have some bad news, Alley," my mother told me as soon as I answered my phone. I held my breath, waiting. "Mr. Wallace passed away."

My heart dropping to my stomach, I did my best to bite back tears as I asked, "What happened?" I wasn't good with death—less good with it when it was spontaneously thrown at me like a spitball.

"A heart attack. His funeral is Saturday. I hope you and Blake can make it. If not, the family understands."

This was typical of my mother. It was her way of letting me know, if I couldn't handle it, she'd make an excuse for me; but of course we would be there. We were talking about sweet, old Mr. Wallace who taught me how to play poker and always let me win. I wouldn't miss it. I'd do what I had to do to mentally prepare myself for his spitball funeral.

"We'll be there, Mom."

* * *

Blake was able to switch shifts with one of the guys at the station to have Saturday morning off. I was glad. I needed him. I was really feeling off-kilter. My routine had gone to shit, and I felt out of control. Blake was my constant; he had been since we met. In a strange way, he saved me from myself.

Blake had pulled me over after I stopped in the middle of the road to let a cat cross the street. He acknowledged how very nice that was of me, but cited a dead stop in the middle of the road could have caused an accident. Full-heartedly agreeing that it wasn't the smartest thing I ever did, I was quick to point out we were talking about a cat and there was no one behind me. I used these fine points to barter for a warning over the ticket I thought he was itching to write. To my surprise, he'd said, "Instead of a warning, how about dinner?'"

I've always been a sucker for the light eyes, dark hair combo. Blake being a cop made the proposal that much sweeter. Going from a short order cook to a man in a uniform felt nothing short of a miracle.

Blake was a by-the-book kind of guy. More so when it came to him being a police officer. He didn't bend the law. The only time he drives over the speed limit is when he's on call. He's the perfect little soldier in blue. It's hard to believe he'd hit on a girl he pulled over. It was his one blemish on his moral police record. But as he told me all the time: 'You were worth it'. He would break the law for me, and only me, over and over again. Not that hitting on me was breaking a law, but it was definitely in the sexual harassment category.

Sure, Blake and I had our fights and like any couple—we had issues we had to work through—but Blake was and would always be my rock.

Like most women, before I found Mr. Right, I dated a football team of Mr. Wrongs. Most of them didn't think my quirks were cute. My need for pause was annoying, strange, or my favorite lackluster complaint: stupid. The only guy besides Blake that could handle my so-called quirks was Billy. But with Billy things got intense. He was *Where's Waldo* clingy. If he wasn't physically with me, he'd be in the background just waiting for me to pinpoint him out of the crowd. Whether it was at the grocery store or while out to lunch with my mother, Billy would just pop up out of the blue.

Things had gotten creepy fast with Billy. Catching him going through my phone was just the reason I needed to give him the axe. Men with Billy's kind of intensity had to be delt with delicately. A breakup for no good reason wouldn't result in a breakup. The breach of privacy was breakup-worthy and I used it as my *Excalibur*, liberating myself from yet another bad boyfriend.

In the beginning, Billy had been great, but like most good things, they have to come to an end so you can find something better. And that better was Blake Durwood, the father of my soon-to-be born twins and officer of the year.

Blake took my hand as we walked passed Mr. Wallace's open casket. He looked peaceful. I was grateful for that. He didn't look dead—not really—just in a deep, deep sleep.

As we continued our procession past the casket my eyes landed on a flower arrangement made of spring-colored posies. In the center of this wreath of sweet-smelling flowers was a card. From the imperfection of the drawing and the rough texture of the crayons used in its rendering, I assumed the card was handmade by a child.

What had me pausing to think was the subject matter drawn on the front of the card. It wasn't flowers, or a heart, or anything you think a child would draw on a sympathy card. No—on this handmade card was a pig, drawn with the stereotypical round nose and face. Quickly, I ruled out the possibility that I was looking at a pink dog. The pig on the card had the iconic corkscrew tail. It was without a doubt, unequivocally, a pig.

I hadn't given much thought, if any, to the strange five-dollar bill I had found at the park a few days earlier. I filed it away under *weird* and went about my routine. But when something bothers you, you never really forget it; it's just hibernating in the recesses of your mind.

All of the strangeness of that day rushed back into my head in a migraine. "Greed is a sin, and you just let me in," I mumbled under my breath, my sleeping memory waking from its dormancy. My entire body felt hot as my mind wheeled. This card was here for me to see. I was sure of it. I felt it in my bones. "Look," I whispered to Blake.

"Cute," he said. "It must be from one of the grandkids."

I pulled the card from the arrangement, opening it to read: YOU LET ME INTO YOUR LIFE AND I HUFFED, AND I PUFFED, AND I BLEW ON YOUR HEART.

"Blake," I panted, my heartbeat traveling to my head, my temples pulsating like speakers. "Read this!"

"That's sweet."

"Sweet?!" I barked, my lips pulling back in what I knew had to be an ugly display of teeth. "What's wrong with you?! It's a murder confession. What are you, the worst cop ever?!"

His lips flattened as he clenched his jaw, the muscle running up his cheek twitching.

I had crossed a line. "Sorry," I said hurriedly, full of remorse. Why do we always hurt the ones we love most? I always went from one to a hundred at a turn of a dime. "You know I didn't mean that," I said, dropping my voice to barely a whisper.

"I'm not a detective Alley, but that is *not* a murder confession," he said in a no-nonsense tone. Blake got like that every now and again—really, really, serious. When his temperament became severe it was like his mood pervaded everything, making everyone and everything quiet. The chatter between the mourners and the low-grade whimpers disappeared. There was only us.

I approached the subject with caution. "Look at the handwriting. It matches the message on the five-dollar bill from the park. It's written in all caps and it's another *Three Little Pigs* reference, which *you* pointed out in the first place. The card is talking about the Big Bad Wolf. He huffed, and he puffed and he—"

Blake cut me off, finishing my sentence, "Blew the house down. The card says heart, not house."

"Well, the killer couldn't cause an earthquake, but they *could* cause a heart attack. What did you call the last message—metaphorical?"

Blake took the card from me and placed it back in the flower arrangement. "Come on, we're holding up the line."

Saying nothing, my hand stiff in his, we took a seat at the back of the funeral parlor.

He whispered in my ear, "I know what you're thinking Al, but it's nothing."

"If it's nothing, why are you drawing the same conclusion?"

"Alley Cat, you know I love you. You know that, but you see things differently. You're brain connects things in a different way."

"I'm autistic Blake, not crazy," I seethed, louder than I meant to. The couple in the seats in front of us turned around and glared. I faked an apologetic smile. Satisfied with this, they turned around and went back to grieving.

"I know that," Blake said, keeping his tone even. He was very good at not getting upset with me. Blake had the patience of a saint. I knew he would be an excellent father. "Mr. Wallace died of a heart attack, Al. He wasn't murdered. I know it seems like it would make things easier to have someone to blame, but there's no one. Mr. Wallace had health issues, that's why he walked at the park every day. Whoever wrote the card simply meant that Mr. Wallace had touched their heart and likewise, they did the same. End of story."

CHAPTER THREE

The Return of the Big Bad Wolf

Monday hit and I was back on track. My daily routine was in full swing, and I felt much better for it. I figured Blake was as much on edge as I was, having skipped our walks on the weekend. He was an exercise junkie. Lifting weights in the morning wasn't enough to get his blood pumping. He jogged during his lunch break and strolled with me after work. Blake was as happy as a pig-in-shit as we took the same old walk around the park and saw the same old faces, minus the Wallaces. That was one change I was going to have to get used to, whether I liked it or not. Mr. Wallace wasn't coming back.

As we passed the visitor center to get to the parking lot, I suddenly stopped dead in my tracks. My chest ached as if an invisible phantom was squeezing my heart. For a second, I thought I was going to join Mr. Wallace.

There was a face-up five-dollar bill next to the welcome sign of the park. It was in the same vicinity, if not in the exact same spot as the last five-dollar bill I found there. To add to the tightness that was spreading like a deep freeze from my heart to my extremities, the money wasn't there when we started our walk. I had checked. In the back of my abnormal little brain, I had thought it would be there. When it wasn't, I laughed in relief at my overactive imagination. But it was there now, as plain as the pig nose drawn on President Lincoln's face.

"Blake," I gasped, pointing.

His face twisted, his calm demeanor cracking in front of me like an egg. "There's no way it's the same one," he said with less than his usual confidence.

"Because Mr. Wallace put it in his pocket, right?"

He thought about it for a moment before he answered. "Yeah Al, we saw him."

"We should make sure. I see the pig face, let's see if it has the same message." Crouching to get a better look, I used a small stick to unfold the corner of the bill. The peach fuzz on my arms bristled. A wave of déjà vu rippled up my spine to my brain. It was the same message, written the same way—in all capital letters—like you'd expect to see in a serial killer documentary.

Blake went to pick it up. "Don't touch it," I said in a near-shout.

He picked it up anyway. "There's no way it's the same one. We saw Mr. Wallace put it in his pocket and it would've blown away over the weekend if he'd left it here," he muttered to himself.

Blake flipped the five over, examining both sides of it.

"What are you thinking?" I asked.

He clicked his tongue before he answered. "Some kid probably made a whole bunch of these and is just fucking with people. The question is, how far are they taking it?" Using his hand as a sun visor, Blake surveyed the park.

"What do you mean?"

"We could be a mark. Us, or any poor sucker who picks up the five."

"A mark?" I asked, my face wrinkling at the word. "What's that?" Instinctively, my arms wrapped around the twins. I didn't like the sound of that.

"Whoever put this here is close enough to watch us. It's no fun if they can't see our reaction. It's a game to them. They watch and wait to see who takes the bait, and then follow them home."

I joined Blake in combing over the park. "Does that mean you think Mr. Wallace was followed home?"

"Maybe," he said, his eyes scanning the cars in the parking lot.

The park was empty for a Monday. Rain was forecasted but it never came. The bogus weather report resulted in only a few people scattered in the park with about half a dozen cars in the parking lot.

"We could ask Billy," I suggested, my eyes cutting to Big Bill's Homemade Water Ice food truck in the parking lot.

Blake knew I had dated Billy, but that was about all he knew. I didn't let on how serious we'd been or that, like the Wallaces, Billy had been a staple in my life for better or worse, owing to the fact he grew up in the house on the other side of my parents and still lived at home.

These days, I made it a point to only wave hello and goodbye to Billy, never stopping to chat, but this occasion was worth all the awkwardness in the world. Fiancé and ex could tolerate each other for a few minutes.

Billy was a permanent fixture at Batsto Park—if anyone saw anything out of the ordinary, it would be him. He was always there, rain or shine, now that he had taken up the mantle from his father. I heard it through the grapevine that Billy's dad was suffering from early-onset dementia. It's a shame; Big Bill, aka Mr. McCormick, was always very nice. The news of his diagnosis was just one of the recent blows to the McCormick family.

Right before Mr. McCormick's dementia became public knowledge, in the way all things do in a small town, Billy had been arrested for drug possession. After he got out of prison, Billy was literally in the driver's seat of his family's business, which—thanks to his stint in jail—had suffered. I wasn't sure what people thought. It wasn't like Billy was putting razor blades in the Italian ice, but small towns were like that. Once you were labeled, you're labeled, and good luck climbing out of that box.

I'm not going to lie—I was surprised when I heard Billy got arrested. Prior to him becoming OCD with my every move, Billy had been a nice guy. It's why I'd dated him. He seemed like the whole package: nice and good looking, with a soft side that let him enjoy poetry and chick flicks. Sure, he vaped the occasional joint, but I never saw him partake in anything illegal, and certainly not the hard drugs he was arrested for. Luckily for Billy, it was his first offense, and the judge went easy on him.

I'd spoken to Billy a few times after he got out of prison. I wanted him to know I didn't shun him as a pariah like most of the town. There had been bad blood between us, but there had been a lot of good too. I wasn't into cancel culture. We're all human. We all make mistakes, and with that we all deserve a second chance. Billy and I could and would never be an item again, but I had been optimistic we could be cordial, if not friends again one day. However, once things got serious with Blake, I thought it was best to just stick to my Miss America wave. No new boyfriend wanted to see his girl buddy-buddy with her ex-boyfriend. I was sure on some level Billy understood. He never pressed to talk to me. He would just wave back, and just like that, things continued to move along according to my routine.

Blake's light eyes cut to the food truck. "No."

I huffed, feeling like the Big Bad Wolf. "Why not?"

"He probably didn't see anything."

"We won't know that until we ask, and you just said the money left on the ground could be a sicko's invitation to follow someone home. This is serious; we should ask Billy."

"I was wrong," Blake told me with such indifference it made me immediately suspicious.

My eyes narrowed. "Why the sudden change of heart?"

"I jumped to conclusions. I shouldn't have said anything. I didn't mean to scare you." He rubbed my arm. "I'm sorry."

"I'm not scared; I'm paranoid and I'm asking Billy," I defiantly announced, yanking the five-dollar bill out of Blake's hand and strolling over to the food truck.

"I'll do it," Blake conceded, catching up to me with a few large strides. "I don't want you talking to him."

"Fine," I huffed, handing him back the five. "You do it."

Billy was facing away from the window, busy cooking what had to be French fries as we approached the food truck. The smell of greasy potatoes made my mouth water. I craved fries before I was pregnant, but now the craving was primal. I needed French fries like I needed air.

A rattling sound filled the parking lot as Blake knocked on the side panel of the food truck. "Hey, Billy, you have a moment?"

Billy turned around, evidently surprised to see us, his blue eyes going wide. "Oh, hey." He narrowed in on me. "Alley, so good to see you."

"You too, Billy."

"How have you been? Busy, I guess," he said, his eyes lowering to my round belly.

Like a well-practiced soon to be mother, I placed my hand over the twins. "You could say that."

"I like the names you picked out. Your mom told my dad."

"Cute, right?"

Making himself known, Blake cleared his throat. "Billy, have you seen anything or anyone suspicious around the park?"

"Define suspicious, officer. It's hard to know who to trust these days. In my experience, you can't trust family or the law. It's like the Wild West here in Pleasant Mills."

I wasn't sure if Billy's less than helpful attitude was because Blake was my fiancé or because Blake was a cop, and after his time in jail all cops were bad cops. I was thinking it was the latter; there was no way Billy still held a torch for me. We'd dated years ago.

Although, his father did tell my mother recently that Billy still believes that I am *the one.* I wondered if he still thought that now that he had a good look at my two buns in the oven.

"Excuse me a moment," Billy said, turning his attention to the fries. He pulled them out of the fryer and put them in a paper carrier.

"Show him the five," I said to Blake.

Billy handed me the piping hot fries. "Don't worry about it," Billy said. "For you, Alley, it's free."

"Thanks, but I meant we found a five-dollar bill we wanted to ask you about."

His eyebrows reached his hairline. "Oh, okay, but, uh, the fries are still on the house. I was just making them for myself."

Blake handed him the five we found as I dug into the fries. They were golden greasy perfection. This was one bump in my routine I was happy about. By now I was used to serving my food cravings. They were my masters and I their meager servant.

Billy grinned, looking over the five-dollar bill. "Quite the artist," he remarked dryly.

"And poet," I added.

His already light eyes brightened as he beamed at me. "Touché."

"So, let's have it Billy, have you seen anyone over by the visitor's center that's not a regular? You see anyone purposely drop that bill? Or others like it?"

He shook his head, his dark locks falling over his forehead.

"Has anyone paid with a bill like this?"

Billy's head swayed back and forth as if he was a bobble head glued to the dashboard of a Jeep speeding through mud puddles.

"Can you check?" Blake asked in his no-nonsense tone.

The register door opened with a high-pitched ding. Billy pulled out a small stack of fives and showed us. "Sorry, I can't help. What's this all about anyway?"

Blake took the doodled on five back and put it in his wallet. I was going to protest and say we should leave it where we found it, but I didn't want to make a scene in front of Billy. He handed Billy five singles. "For the fries."

"If I notice anything strange, I'll give you a ring." His eyes locked with mine. "Take care of yourself, Alley."

"Thank you for your time," Blake said, wrapping his arm around my shoulders and turning me around.

"No problem, what are old friends for?" Billy called after us.

"We need to put it back, just in case," I whispered to Blake as we walked away from the food truck.

"I know," he agreed.

We headed back to the visitor center and Blake placed the five-dollar bill on the ground where we had found it.

"I have an idea. Hold this," I said, handing him my fries. "If some jerk is watching and waiting, they're going to be waiting a long time—a *Rip Van Winkle* century." I used a stick to dig a small hole in the ground and buried the five. "Greed is a sin, and I just buried it with a stick, you dick."

Standing up, I dusted my hands on the tops of my thighs. "How's that for prophetic poetry?"

I wasn't sure what Blake said in response, or if he even responded. My eyes had naturally drifted to the food truck where Billy was watching us with a smile plastered on his face. I gave him my calculated wave. He waved back, his grin widening.

CHAPTER FOUR
All the Way Home

Sitting down at the kitchen table, I opened the day's mail on autopilot. Most of it was junk mail, advertising all the things a bride couldn't be without. Some were bills and some were cards from friends and family who weren't going to be able to make it to the wedding. I opened a white envelope, thinking I was going to find another *Sorry-can't-make-it*, when I pulled out a card with a hand-drawn pig on it. It was just like the one at Mr. Wallace's funeral. With trembling hands, my chest ballooning, I opened it to read: *HERE PIGGY, PIGGY, PIGGY. GREED IS A SIN, AND THERE'S MORE THAN ONE WAY TO LET ME IN. YOU TOOK SOMETHING THAT WASN'T YOURS AND NOW THE BIG BAD WOLF WILL BE KNOCKING AT YOUR DOOR.*

Frantically, I turned the envelope around to see who the card was from. There was no stamp, no post mark, no sender's address. The envelope was left in the mailbox and was addressed to Blake by his full legal name: To Pete Blakefield Durwood, the piggy in the brick house.

My heart was beating fast—too fast. It felt like it was going to beat right out of my heaving chest onto the kitchen table. The Big Bad Wolf knew where we lived. He had come as close as the mailbox, maybe closer.

I dialed Blake, gooseflesh enveloping my entire body. I could be such a narcissist sometimes. The five-dollar bill and its ominous message wasn't left in the park for me to find. I wasn't the mark, Blake was. Piggy—Pig—that was a slur reserved for cops.

* * *

Blake had been a police officer for five years, and in that time had mostly just handed out speeding tickets. There had been a few domestic calls, but he didn't think any of the people involved would've held a grudge against him.

Detective Weston thought it was likely that the card was sent out of a vendetta. Blake, not harboring ill will, meant diddly-squat. The Pleasant Mills police department could be dealing with a real psychopath. A psychopath that knew where we lived. A psychopath that knew we walked in the park every evening. The nut probably knew our entire schedule, thanks to my need to stick to a routine. Here I was, Ms. Predictable, putting my fiancé in danger.

A cop—one of Blake's friends—was put on surveillance. It didn't make me feel very safe. We lived on a wooded lot, tall trees surrounding us like a peninsula. What if the Big Bad Wolf came from the woods, bypassing the cop waiting across the street in the more than conspicuous government vehicle? I wasn't taking my chances. With the wedding a few days away and my stress level at its max, I headed to my parents' house.

The temporary relocation only helped a little. My parents' house was in a development, so that eliminated invasion from the woods; but if I was right and the card at Mr. Wallace's funeral was from the Big Bad Wolf, he had most likely already put together that my parents lived next door to the Wallaces. He was targeting Blake, not me, but I would bet the hair on my chinny-chin-chin that didn't matter to someone suffering from that kind of crazy.

What did make me feel a little better was the fact that my

father was a retired Marine, and he would be home with my mother. In addition, I would be sandwiched between Mrs. Wallace and the McCormick family.

I felt safer in numbers, even if Billy was a person of interest. He was so because of me, because of Blake and me. When Blake and a handful of other police officers went to retrieve the five-dollar bill I buried, it was gone, landing Billy in a world of trouble. He had watched me bury it, a thing he readily admitted to the Pleasant Mills Police Department, but he denied digging it up. Blake didn't believe him, and I wasn't sure if I did. Blaming Billy would be the easy option. If I could have been there when they questioned him, been a fly on the wall and saw his reaction, maybe I could have gauged his honesty, even his innocence.

There was a teeny tiny part of me, perhaps a larger part of me than I cared to admit, that thought it was possible the card wasn't talking about the five-dollar bill, but was alluding to me when it said: *YOU TOOK SOMETHING THAT WASN'T YOURS.* I was what Blake took from Billy. But he wouldn't hurt me, not Billy. And Billy wouldn't harass Blake. This whole thing was making me crazy. Billy was just trying to move on with his life; I wish the universe would let him. But then again, Billy's smile that day in the park had haunted my sleep and waking hours—the way it had curved in a knowing grin, the way his teeth seemed too sharp.

CHAPTER FIVE
A Brick House

The entire Pleasant Mills Police Department was at our wedding in some capacity, either as a guest or on surveillance. I did my best to have a good time, and I did, but there was something with us the whole night. At any given moment, I would glance over my shoulder, the little hairs on the nape of my neck bristling for no reason.

"It's your mind playing tricks on you," Blake whispered to me, catching me staring at nothing.

I knew he was right. I was safe; well, for the night. Yesterday, he had told me the surveillance had to stop. After the wedding we were to move back into our house and get back to our routine. The local police department didn't have the manpower for around the clock babysitting, and we couldn't go on living scared.

It looked like Blake was right from the beginning and the so-called Big Bad Wolf was just a prankster getting his jollies out of frightening people. He knew our schedule and where we lived; if his intention was to hurt us, he would have already. His mission was to scare us. Mission accomplished; he should be onto his next mark.

The police surveillance was coming to an end. However, the Big Bad Wolf was still a person of interest in Mr. Wallace's heart attack. Rumors he had been scared to death were spreading through town like wildfire. If found, the Big Bad Wolf would be questioned, and according to Blake, would most likely only end up with a slap on the wrist misdemeanor. Scaring someone to death would be a hard thing to prove.

Maybe it was the hormones talking, but hearing from Blake and Detective Weston that we weren't in immediate danger didn't make me feel safe. The facts remained the same: the Big Bad Wolf knew where we lived and had threatened Blake. Like a lot of things in my life, I had to make myself okay with it. It was just another road bump I had to get over: visualize and jump.

From the other side of the room, I watched Blake as he glided across the dance floor with Mrs. Wallace. He spun her around like she was a ballerina, passing her off to another police officer before powwowing with Detective Weston. Blake took a pen from Weston and feverishly scribbled something on a napkin. My heart immediately picked up tempo, my eyes scanning the room for someone who wasn't supposed to be there.

Blake hurriedly approached me. I couldn't appreciate how handsome he looked in his tux, his blue eyes so bright. My nerves were getting the best of me. "What is it?! What did Detective Weston say?! What's going on?! What's on the napkin?!"

He pressed a kiss to my cheek. "Easy Alley Cat, everything is great. Weston has a cabin in the Poconos and he's letting us use it this weekend. I dropped my phone and cracked the screen this morning, hence the napkin. My phone's nothing more than an expensive paperweight; but don't worry, I'll get a new one tomorrow. They have a decent one at Boost Mobile for around a hundred bucks."

"The Poconos this weekend?" I asked, my excitement reaching my voice.

A smile bloomed across his face. "Yeah, isn't that great? It's a sweet little Airbnb. He had a last-minute cancellation, so he's giving it to us."

I tugged on Blake's arm excitedly. I couldn't be mad about his phone. With the wedding and the twins on the way, we didn't have money for a real honeymoon. I had a hard time staying at hotels. It made me feel like a rat trapped in one of many cages. It was just another one of my quirks. But a cabin in the Poconos—that sounded great. It was too warm to ski, but I was sure there were plenty of other things to do.

I didn't have a lot of time to mentally prepare, but it was either the Poconos or going home to our unsupervised house where, now more than ever, the dark woods seemed to swallow our little brick farmhouse. I would make myself okay with the sudden change of plans; in fact, I welcomed it. I kissed Blake back, happy with the news and happy with my flexibility. It would be perfect.

* * *

My parents cleared out for the night so Blake and I could have their house to ourselves. Tomorrow—or rather, after a weekend in the Poconos—things would go back to normal. But for tonight, we were where I felt safest.

My father knew I wasn't carrying another Immaculate Conception, but the idea of shagging like a rabbit with your father in the next room was less than romantic. With my parents happily in a suite in Harrah's and me in a place I was familiar with, we could both have a great night.

And tonight was going to be one for the books. I went all out with a skimpy, strappy, leathery thing that was advertised as lingerie. Usually, I didn't go for that kind of thing, but with it being our wedding night and with everything we'd been through the last two weeks, Blake deserved it. With all of the effort I was putting into getting the ridiculous thing on, I hoped it would live up to his kinky X-rated fantasy. How hot I looked in it at almost five months pregnant was definitely up for debate, but Frederick's of Hollywood had a reputation to withhold, so I trusted in that.

I had just slipped an old button-down nightgown on over my getup when I heard muffled voices. Opening the bathroom door, I detected the voices were coming from downstairs.

Hugging the staircase, I made my way down the steps. "Blake?" Blake came down the hall toward me. "Who were you talking to?"

"Billy."

I felt my eyebrows converge as if by magnetic force. "Why was Billy here?"

He hugged me to him, planting a kiss on my neck. "That guy's loco. I'll be glad when we're rid of him."

My face wrinkled. I was going to need more than that. "What did he want?"

"He wanted to make sure you were okay. I told him not to worry about it, that I'll take care of you. And if he wanted to play guard dog while I made love to you, to be my guest."

Playfully, I slapped Blake's chest. "I hope you didn't say it like that."

A grin highlighted his cheek bones and that dimple in his chin I loved so much. Eagerly, he unbuttoned my night shirt. "Actually, I was a little bit cruder. I said *when I fuck my wife's brains out.*"

"I *really* hope you didn't say that."

He had me out of my night shirt. "Wow, you look smoking hot. The more I'm thinking about it," he said, pressing another kiss to my neck, "the more I'm thinking we should can the trip to the Poconos and maybe just spend the weekend in bed."

"Maybe you're right," I said, taking his hand. "It would be nice to just start our new life."

"I do miss our routine," Blake hankered, letting me lead him to the stairs. He suddenly let go of my hand and headed into the kitchen. "One sec, I need to write something down while it's on my mind. You know how it is—there one second, gone the next."

Waiting for him at the foot of the stairs, I felt a little deflated. "What's so important it can't wait?"

My temper continued to mount, as I listened to him rummaging through the junk drawer in the kitchen, no doubt in search for a pen.

"I wanted to remind myself to get a new phone. I have a feeling we are both going to forget," he shouted.

Blake shut the kitchen lights off and took my hand, pressing a kiss to the top of it. "Sorry about that. Time to make good on what I told Billy," he said with a mischievous smile that was contagious.

"I couldn't agree more," we heard coming from the kitchen, the kitchen lights flashing on. We jerked our heads to see Mr. McCormick as he stepped into the entryway, most of his face cast in shadow, but I would know him anywhere. Billy was the younger version of his father.

As quick as humanly possible, I threw on my night shirt and tried to cover up.

"B—Big Bill," Blake spluttered. "What the hell are you doing here?"

For obvious reasons Billy and his father weren't invited to the wedding.

"You always said you'd die for Billy, and it's collection day. It has to be now. I'm not going to let you get away with it this time, Petey. Not this time."

"Mr. McCormick, I think you're confused," I said in a kind voice. "This is Blake, my fiancé—my husband."

"I know him Al, more than you do."

"You need to go home now, Bill." Blake pulled his cell phone from his pants pocket, audibly sighing over his cracked phone. "Come with me, I'll walk you home."

"I'm not going anywhere, Petey. We have a score to settle."

"Why does he keep calling you that?" I asked.

Before Blake could respond, Mr. McCormick said, "That's his name, you stupid little girl. Pete Durwood. Piggy Pete Blakefield Durwood."

"Piggy Pete," I muttered to myself. I knew Pete was Blake's first name. Of course I knew that—I was Blake's wife. He hated his first name, so he went by his middle name. What I wanted to know was how Mr. McCormick knew that. And I was less than thrilled about the addition of the Piggy moniker.

"Don't talk to her like that," Blake warned. "Like I said, it's time for you to go."

"The poor kid was so fat his own parents called him Piggy Pete. Isn't that right, Petey Boy?"

"Shut up!" Blake shouted, pointing at him, his face flushed a deep scarlet.

"But me, and my wife, and my Billy, we were always good to him. Even after he had his little nervous breakdown and had to be sent away, we still watched out for him. Even after my dear wife passed. Billy was always his best friend. Hell, his only friend. After all our kindness, how does he repay us?"

I placed my hand on Blake's arm, asking in a whisper, "What is he talking about?

"I'll tell you," Mr. McCormick said, his face as flushed as Blake's. "Your breakup with my Billy Boy was his fault. Petey became obsessed with you after Billy showed him a picture of his girlfriend."

"Bill, you need to go home," Blake said in a stern voice.

"Or what? You gonna put Billy in jail again?" I glanced at Blake. His face was as unreadable as stone. "That's right Al," Mr. McCormick went on to say. "Blake, as he likes to go by these days, planted those drugs in Billy's car. He orchestrated the whole thing to get Billy out of the picture so he could make his move on you."

"That's ridiculous," I snapped. "Billy and I broke up before Billy went to jail."

Mr. McCormick waggled his finger at me. "It started before that. Billy was worried about you. Worried Piggy would show up. It's why Billy started following you around and went through your phone. It was for your own protection."

"That's insane," I scoffed, rolling my eyes.

"I wanted to say something for years, from the moment I saw the two of you together, but I had to worry about my own. Billy was in jail, and I wanted him out. He's all I have, and he had to come first. After the stunt Blake just pulled, trying to get Billy arrested for harassing the both of you, I know he won't stop until Billy's behind bars for life."

Mr. McCormick pulled a large hunting knife from his pocket. The blade's edge shone in the dark like a silver slice of the moon. "I have nothing to lose. I'm a lost man. When they find the two of you split open, I'll blame it on the dementia." He mocked-sobbed. "Sorry officers. I'm so sorry. I didn't recognize them. With all the talk around town about a stalker, I thought they were here to hurt Alley and Blake. I didn't know it was them I killed. I swear, all I wanted to do was protect them. I knew Alley since she was a little girl. I loved her like a daughter."

He beckoned to Blake, his smile impossibly wide as he pressed his thumb into his nose to mimic a pig. "Here Piggy, Piggy, Piggy."

I squeezed Blake's arm, my heart beating so loud in my chest it drummed in my head.

"Bill," Blake said with his palms down, trying to diffuse the situation. "You're right, I placed those drugs in Billy's car and I'm sorry. I will turn myself in. Just let Alley go."

Blake's eyes darted toward the front door. I understood. I raced to the door, throwing it open. Billy was waiting on the doorstep, and I found myself in his arms. "Billy, your father!"

"I know," he said, running his hand down my hair, the smell of alcohol wafting off of him like he just bathed in it. "It's going to be okay."

Mr. McCormick froze in place. "Billy Boy, I can explain."

"No need, Pops. I heard it all. I was never positive it was Blake who set me up, but now I know. Did you know, Al?" he asked, holding me in his gaze, his eyes webbed over in red.

I shook my head and whispered so as not to set off Mr. McCormick, who seemed stable for the moment. "I think Blake just said that to appease your dad."

Billy's attention was on Blake. "No Alley, he did it. He's threatened by me. He may have lost a shit ton of weight and gone to college, and got a respectable job, but he will always be Piggy Pete, and I will always be better than him."

"Fuck you!" Blake shouted. "You're a piece of white trash. I didn't want you around her."

"Alley was *my* girlfriend," Billy yelled.

"Not anymore. She's my wife!"

"That's right," Billy mused, his eyes cutting to me. "Congrats, Al."

Things were escalating fast. My phone was upstairs, and I didn't want to risk walking past Mr. McCormick. One wrong word could have him wielding his knife like a samurai. "Um, thanks," I mumbled. I went to push past Billy and have Mrs. Wallace call the police, but was stopped. "Billy, let me by."

"Not this time, Alley. You're not getting a free pass." The smell of alcohol on his hot breath made me nauseous, as if by inhaling his stale exhale I was becoming intoxicated myself. "There was a time, not that long ago, that I'd do anything for you, but now . . ." he muttered, his eyes landing on my round belly. "But now you're his, and those things growing inside of you are his, too. Like my dad said, it's time to even the score. I'm going to cut them out Alley, one at a time, while *Officer Durwood* watches. Then I'm gonna cut him open too, just like the little piggy he is."

"And when it's all done. I'll tell the police I did it," Mr. McCormick said. "They can lock me up, for all the good it will do. In another year, I won't remember my name."

Billy grabbed me by my shoulders, pushing me back into the house. "Squeal little piggy," he said in a voice he had never used with me before.

"Don't you fucking touch her," Blake shouted, coming to my rescue as Mr. McCormick approached with his knife.

"Don't kill him, Dad. Alley has to be first. Petey has to suffer."

Placing my hands over my belly, I shouted at the top of my lungs. "Wait! Wait, Billy! The twins aren't Blake's!"

Everyone froze. It was like someone pushed pause on a television. It was so quiet. I wondered if I screamed, if Mrs. Wallace would hear me. I doubted it. Only I could save my babies, and this was my one chance. Laurel and Harvey were counting on me. Billy was not only punch drunk on whatever alcoholic beverage he'd just binged, but on his father's psycho plan for revenge. This wasn't Billy. He thought the world had turned against him, me included. I just had to flip the script in a way his inebriated brain could understand. "The twins aren't Blake's," I repeated, tears streaming down my cheeks.

Blake's face was pale in the dim light. "W . . . what?!" he stammered.

"I'm sorry, Blake. I wanted to tell you, but I couldn't." I turned to Billy. "They're your father's, Billy. He raped me when I was at my parents' house, watering their plants when they were on vacation. I didn't tell anyone because I was ashamed."

Billy's eyes became alive, burning with a blue fire. He

looked like a wild animal, seething, foaming at the mouth.

"Lying cunt," Mr. McCormick spit.

"It's true, Billy," I said, keeping my eyes glued to his. "It's the reason I stopped talking to you. I couldn't bear it; you looked too much like your father. It wasn't Blake who kept us apart, it was your father. He's to blame."

Billy's eyes cut to his dad, his lips curling back over his teeth like a rabid dog as he lunged at his father.

Blake grasped my hand, and together we raced out into the cool night. He went to his patrol car and grabbed his spare gun out of the trunk. "Go to Mrs. Wallace's house and call the police," he ordered.

I didn't listen. I followed Blake back into my parents' house, the thought of Blake being overpowered painting a gruesome image in my mind.

"Alley, I thought I told you to go next door."

"It's quiet," I whispered. "Too quiet."

"I agree," Blake said, nibbling on his bottom lip. "Stay behind me."

We followed a trail of blood like breadcrumbs down the entry hall to the kitchen. Father and son had killed themselves. They lay together on the tiled floor in a strange embrace of arms and legs, their blood pooling around them in a red lake. The dead resembled each other so much it was as if the past and present had collided in a cruel twist of fate, their blue eyes the same mangled soul.

I took Blake's hand, my heart still galloping as I breathed in the stench of blood. The smell was so thick, there was a metallic taste in the air. There was nothing I could do to help the McCormicks, but I could put Blake's mind at ease. "It was a lie. Mr. McCormick never touched me. I was just trying to get Billy on our side."

He squeezed my hand. "I'm sorry I didn't tell you Billy was

my cousin and that you were my big crush. I was afraid if you knew, you'd think I was crazy."

"I just hope crazy doesn't run in the family," I said, only half kidding. Billy was drunk. I'd been wasted before, but I'd never thought carving up an ex was a good idea. There was clearly something underlyingly wrong with Billy and his father.

Blake pulled a napkin from his pocket and wiped my tears. "Craziness, no. Greed, yes," he admitted, holding me in the frame of his dark lashes. "Greed is one sin I'm guilty of. I wanted you all to myself."

The message from the Big Bad Wolf replayed in my head: *GREED IS A SIN, AND YOU JUST LET ME IN.* Why did Blake have to use that word? It was like cutting open a still-festering wound. My eyes flickered to the red lake on the kitchen floor that had grown into a sea. "Looks like you got your wish. I'm all yours. Mr. McCormick was the Big Bad Wolf and he's dead, and Billy is too."

"Maybe. I better check to see if they're still alive." Blake tucked his gun into the back of his pants before crouching to feel for Mr. McCormick's pulse.

"With that much blood, I doubt it," I sniffed, flipping the napkin over to look for a dry spot to dab my eyes. My pulse jumped, sending my already taxed heart into palpitations. Written on the napkin in all caps, in the same handwriting as the Big Bad Wolf read: REMEMBER TO TAKE YOUR MEDS AND CANCEL POCONOS TRIP.

At that moment, I knew all I needed to know. Glancing up to see Blake covering Billy's mouth and nose with the palm of his hand was just confirmation. Blake—not Mr. McCormick—was the Big Bad Wolf. Mr. McCormick had told the truth about Blake planting the drugs in Billy's car. The money left in the park and the cards were designed to get rid of Billy. As Billy's last breath rattled in his chest, Blake completed his mission.

"They're both dead," Blake announced, joining me by my side.

I handed him the napkin, a fire growing in my chest. I wanted him to know I knew.

"Did you write this?" he asked, his brows furrowing into a deep crease.

I was sure my face mirrored his. He seemed genuinely surprised by the message on the napkin. "What? No! You did it. It's your napkin."

He shook his head, flipping the napkin over to show me the address for the cabin in the Poconos and a reminder to get a new phone. "No, I wrote this." He scrutinized me with his eyes. "You can't tell me you think I'm the one who wrote those messages in the park and the cards!"

I said nothing. My mind was spinning like a merry-go-round; everything was blurring together.

"Alley, you know my handwriting, and I don't take meds."

"I don't know what it looks like in all caps," I said, studying him, waiting to see if his mask cracked. It was true he didn't take medication, but 'meds' could be police code for Tylenol.

"Al," he pleaded, reaching for my hand.

I recoiled.

"Al, Alley cat, you know me. Billy and his dad were bad news. Tonight proved that. Hell, yeah, I wanted Billy gone, but not so badly I'd scare you to do it. What kind of man do you take me for?"

"A man who planted drugs in their cousin's car."

His eyes narrowed to slits. "I admit I set Billy up. I was a young cop, and it was a mistake, but I would never ever deliberately hurt you or the twins. If you want me to turn myself in, I will."

"Oh my," Mrs. Wallace said from the hall. "This is quite the mess, and all over your mother's new floor."

In unison, our heads snapped in Mrs. Wallace's direction, where she appeared as a looming shadow in the hallway. "You poor thing. You must be scared out of your wits. I thought I heard yelling, but with my hearing I couldn't be sure. Come here child, I'll make it all better."

"Mrs. Wallace," I sobbed, fresh tears gushing from my sore eyes. I went to run to her, but Blake yanked me back. At the same time, he pulled his gun from his pants and fired a shot. The ringing in my ears drowned out the sound of Mrs. Wallace as she collapsed onto the floor.

"Blake, what the hell are you doing?!"

He stopped me from rushing to Mrs. Wallace, securing me in a bear hug. "Wait, Alley. Let me make sure she's dead."

I pounded on his chest. "What's wrong with you, you maniac, that's Mrs. Wallace!"

"Alley," he said in his stern voice. "You need to calm down."

"You killed Billy and Mrs. Wallace!"

"Billy's father killed him, not me."

"I saw you smother him with your palm."

"He had no pulse. I was checking to see if I felt breath."

"And Mrs. Wallace, what about her?! You killed her!" I sobbed.

Blake firmly grasped my hand and led me out into the hall. He flipped on the light and said in a calm voice, "Look, Alley. Take a good look."

I pawed at my tears, my eyes widening. Mrs. Wallace was flat on her back, her arms and legs sprawled at her sides. There was a dark spot, smack-dab in the middle of her forehead. Blake had fired the perfect shot, but that wasn't the thing that silenced me. In her right hand was a gun.

"I saw the glint of her gun and put it all together. Look at her outfit, Alley. It's the middle of the night. If she rushed over here because she thought she heard you scream, she would have been wearing pajamas. And the napkin—I had been dancing with Mrs. Wallace before I got the address for the Airbnb from Weston. I must have gotten the napkin from her. And as far as what she wrote on it, it proves she canceled her reservation last minute, knowing Weston would offer it to us for our honeymoon. Mr. Wallace passed away last week, but yet she waited until our wedding night to cancel her reservation. Think about it, Alley. I think Mrs. Wallace was planning on making her move this weekend, but having heard a commotion she decided to act now when she could blame our deaths on the McCormicks."

"I don't understand," I panted. "Why would Mrs. Wallace want to hurt you?"

He tucked my hair behind my ears. "Not me, Alley, you. It was like I said from the beginning, the message on the five-dollar bill was metaphorical. As far as letting greed in, she was talking about lust. Greed comes in all flavors: money, power, food, passion."

I rubbed at my eyes. "She was really upset when the news broke I was pregnant before the wedding."

He dragged his thumbs under my eyes to dry my tears. "That's right, she was. She's been a Bible bumper for so long it warped her brain. Mr. Wallace must have found out what she was up to, and it killed him."

"And that's what the card sent to the house meant. She blamed me for her husband's death. *YOU TOOK SOMETHING THAT WASN'T YOURS*—she thought I took him from her."

He nodded, somberly.

I glanced at Billy and Mr. McCormick before finding my way back to Mrs. Wallace. The dark spot on her forehead had spread over her face and into her open eyes and mouth.

"You really can't choose your neighbors, can you?" I asked.

A smile played on Blake's lips. "It's a good thing the only neighbors we have at our house are trees."

I threw my arms around Blake. "I love you so much. So, so much. Let's go home."

Hugging me tightly, he whispered, "I've always loved you Alley, and I always will. Remind me to call and cancel the Airbnb tomorrow."

* * *

I went upstairs to pack our things while Blake waited downstairs for the police and ambulance. Having packed all of my belongings at warp speed, I decided to pack for Blake.

Grabbing his gym bag from the closet, I tossed it onto the bed. My eyebrows pitched at the odd sound of rattling. I searched through Blake's bag looking for the source of the unusual sound. In the inner zippered compartment, I found a little orange pill bottle that was nearly full.

The label had been blacked out with a marker, but that was no biggie—I knew a life hack for that. I held the pill bottle under the lamp in the bedroom. The pills were donepezil, and they were prescribed to Pete Blakefield. I grabbed my phone, going straight to Google, and discovered that donepezil is a medication used in the treatment of early-onset dementia.

As I thought, I shook the pill bottle like a tambourine. Pete Blakefield was Blake's first and middle name. He was clearly under the care of a doctor, but he made sure to keep it off his medical record by not using his legal name. Early-onset dementia would be an automatic forced retirement from the police. He didn't want them to know, and he didn't want me to know.

Dumbfounded, I sat down on the bed, reading the symptoms of early-onset dementia: memory loss, paranoia, hallucinations, delusions, bizarre behavior. Blake checked off all of those boxes, including every box for holistic approaches to combat the neurological disease: having a healthy lifestyle, exercising daily, and sticking to a routine.

Mental illness did run in the family. Blake had lied to me from the beginning, but I knew he never lied about loving me. His confused mind orchestrated the whole mess to protect me from the McCormicks and the Wallaces.

Billy and his father were bad news. Blake didn't have to tell me that twice. They had come inches within murdering our family. I was glad they were both dead. My tears weren't for them. They were for Blake and me and the twins. I was relieved they were gone and couldn't hurt my family. It was worth Blake scaring me to know I would never have to worry about Billy or his father again.

I realized that when I found the five-dollar bill for the second time, that Blake must have dropped it after we walked by. This way it would be waiting for me to find on our way back to the car. The park was practically dead that day, so there was a good chance I'd be the one to find it, and I did.

Mr. Wallace most likely had a plain, old heart attack and Blake used it to his advantage, or maybe it just fueled his paranoia. I believed Blake when he said he would never hurt me. I think he really was looking for the bad guy, but that bad guy wasn't Mrs. Wallace. It was true she had been very callous when she heard I was pregnant. But she didn't drop in tonight to kill us, and she didn't plan on killing us on our honeymoon. She came to help, but Blake saw her gun and plugged the narrative into the already spiraling delusion playing out in his head.

I hugged my belly and sobbed. This little piggy married the Big Bad Wolf. And this little piggy would remind him to take his medication and remind him to call to cancel the Airbnb in the morning. Blake accepted my quirks, I would accept his. By the hair on my chinny-chin-chin, I would make sure we lived happily ever after in our little brick house.

The End . . .

THANKS FOR READING!

If this book helped you escape, if only for a moment, please consider taking the time to leave a review or star rating on Amazon or whatever platform you use. It would warm the cockles of my little black heart to hear from you.

Looking for something else to read? Don't forget to check out my other books on Amazon.

Follow me on social media (I'm on all platforms under Holly Knightley). Sign up for my newsletter for the latest news, glimpse into my wacky process, and receive the occasional freebie. Stay spooky, and happy reading!

WANT MORE?

CHECK OUT MY OTHER BOOKS!

ABOUT THE AUTHOR

Holly Knightley is a supernatural suspense author and a lifelong devotee of all things macabre, dark, and spooky.

She writes character driven stories that highlight the flaws we all have, delving into the fray of right and wrong and good versus evil. In the thick of nail-nibling mystery and suspense, you will find dark humor that will make you smile in the face of horror.

Holly calls New Jersey home, where she resides with her husband and their four furbabies in a haunted house.

www.ingramcontent.com/pod-product-compliance
Lightning Source LLC
Chambersburg PA
CBHW031453310726
48971CB00003B/894